New

CRASH! STACKS

WITHDRAWN

Scott Shirley
and
Scott Lisetor

A PERSPECTIVES BOOK
High Noon Books
Novato, California

Series Editor: Penn Mullin
Cover Design: Sue Rother
Illustrations: Herb Heidinger

International Standard Book Number: 0-87879-297-X

9 8 7 6 5 4 3 2
20 19 18 17 16 15 14 13

You'll enjoy all the High Noon Books. Write for
a free complete list of titles.

Contents

CHAPTER 1

Alive

They were going to crash! The huge white mountain rushed towards them.

"Heads between your knees!" Dave Bennett yelled from the pilot's seat. Josh and Susan did as their father said. They were cold with fear. Their mother sat stiffly in the copilot's seat. She stared at the mountain coming closer and closer. Suddenly there was a huge roar. Then nothing but blackness!

Susan woke up with the taste of blood in her mouth. She was lying across the back seat of the plane. At that moment, all that was real to her was the pain in her neck and head. She stared up at the sky. A hole had been torn in the roof of the plane. The sun beat down on her face. She shut her eyes. Then she blacked out again. When she awoke again the sun was gone. The taste of blood was still in her mouth. Then she

"Heads between your knees." Suddenly there was a huge roar.

remembered. She remembered Dad yelling. And that terrible noise.

Suddenly she understood. She hadn't died—she had made it through the crash! But Mom, Dad, Josh? There was a cold sick feeling deep inside her. She had to look for them. She had to see if they were all right. Her whole body felt stiff. Would she be able to turn onto her side? Susan held her breath and slowly moved her body.

It was then that she saw Josh. He lay on the floor right below her. She stared at her brother's back. She was afraid to touch him. Her mind was still moving very slowly. Maybe this was good. It kept her from thinking about what might lie ahead. She stared at the rise and fall of Josh's chest. He was alive! She lay there just watching her brother breathe.

Susan looked up at where her parents' seats should be. But the seats had been jerked way forward by the crash. Her parents' bodies were pinned against the plane's control panel! She stared in horror at the backs of their heads. Were they alive? It was impossible to tell. She had to get to them. She opened her mouth to call out. But no words came. She tried again. This time she was able to make a sound.

"Dad! Mom!" Her voice cracked and her throat ached. There was no answer. The two bodies did not move. Susan felt a strange shaking begin in her legs. Her mind was beginning to work again. She was beginning to understand the full horror of what was happening. Were they *all* going to die up here on this mountain?

3

CHAPTER 2

The Survivors

Suddenly Susan heard a sound. It seemed to come from the front of the plane. There it was again—a cough! Susan tried to sit up. Her head felt heavy. She stood up. Everything seemed to be spinning in front of her eyes. She grabbed the wall of the plane to steady herself. Then she carefully stepped over Josh's body. She made her way to the two front seats. One of her parents had coughed. Which one?

Her mother's face was turned towards Susan. It lay pressed against the control panel. Her eyes were closed. There was a long ugly gash on her forehead. Blood ran down along the sides of her face.

"Mom!" Susan knelt down beside Diane. Her mother opened her eyes for a moment. Then she closed them again.

"Mom! You can't die! Wake up! Please! Wake up again!" Her mother's eyes stayed closed. But

Susan could see that she was breathing. That was the important thing.

Susan grabbed onto her father's shoulders. His face was down against the control panel. She tried to pull him up. His head was heavy. It started to fall right back down onto the controls again. His neck seemed to have no strength. Was it broken? Suddenly Susan's hand felt the heartbeat in her father's neck. He was alive! But for how much longer? Susan felt sick with fear. She knew nothing about first aid. She had been meaning to take the class at school last year. But she had put it off.

Susan looked back at where Josh lay on the floor. She could still see his steady breathing.

"Susan." She turned around. Her father had said her name! She grabbed Dave, and they held each other tightly.

Dave was able to sit up straighter now. He reached out towards Diane's limp body in the next seat.

"She's alive, Dad!" Susan said. "She woke up once but then passed out again. Josh hasn't come to at all. I'm scared, Dad."

Dave was trying to get out of his safety belt. Susan started to help him. Suddenly he cried out in pain.

Suddenly Susan's hand felt the heartbeat in her father's neck. He was alive! But for how much longer?

"My leg! I can't move it. I think it's broken." Dave's face was gray with pain. His leg was twisted at a horrible angle.

"Careful, Dad. Don't move any more," Susan said. She felt an awful chill. Dad was supposed to be taking over. He was supposed to be getting them all off the mountain. With a broken leg Dad was helpless. Susan felt more scared than ever before in her life.

There was a sudden move behind Susan. Josh was awake. He was pulling himself up on his elbows.

"Josh! I'm so glad you're OK!" Susan knelt down beside her brother. He stared at her with dazed eyes. Ugly bruises were starting to form all over his face. He must have hit the side wall of the plane in the crash. Dried blood was caked at the corners of his mouth.

Dave called to his son. "Josh, can you hear me? Are you all right?"

"I hear you, Dad," Josh answered weakly. "Where are we? Where's Mom?"

"Mom's still knocked out. She hit her head pretty badly. I've smashed up my leg. What a mess! But we're all alive. That's the main thing," Dave said. "I just wish I'd been able to reach someone on the radio before we went down."

Susan could see that her father was in pain. She knew it was hard for him to talk.

"The plane really held together in the crash. I'm glad we took a bigger plane this time. That's why we all made it," Dave said. He spoke very slowly and softly. "But I don't know where we are." He tried to turn on the plane's radio. It was completely dead, broken in the crash.

CHAPTER 3

Night Is Near

Josh stood up. His head ached. He felt dizzy. He moved slowly towards his mother's seat. She still lay with her head down on the controls. His father sat beside her in the pilot's seat.

"I'll get some blankets, Josh," Susan said. "We should cover them both. I can feel it getting colder." She brought out two wool blankets from the supply box. Josh helped her wrap the blankets around their parents. Susan knew the blankets would not be enough for the long night ahead. They were going to have to make a fire. But where? Not in the plane. Any spilled gas would cause an explosion. They would have to make a shelter away from the plane. It was the only way.

Suddenly Diane began to wake up. She slowly raised her head. Her face was covered with blood. The control panel had cut her in a dozen places. Her eyes looked wildly around the cabin of the plane.

Dave quickly put his arm around her. "It's OK. It's OK. You hit your head and were knocked out. The plane went down, but we all made it. We're all OK."

Josh and Susan hugged their mother. She was still in a daze. She kept touching the cuts on her face. Susan knew they must hurt a lot. They needed to be washed and cleaned.

"I can melt some snow when we start a fire," Susan said. "Then we can take care of those cuts, Mom. I'm going outside and look for a place to build a shelter."

"I'll come with you," Josh said.

"No. Stay here with Mom and Dad. I'll call you when I find a place."

"I think the plane door might be jammed, Susan," Dave said.

"I'll help you open it." Josh and Susan pushed down hard on the door handle. It would not budge. Were they going to have to climb out through the roof? Susan knew they could never get their father out that way. At last the door handle swung down. They shoved open the heavy door. A blast of cold air hit their faces. It was getting dark. They had to get a shelter and fire built soon.

"I'll see you in a minute. I'm not going far from the plane. We could never carry Dad very far," Susan said. She pulled on her ski jacket and gloves.

"Be careful, Susan," her father called to her. "Stay near the plane. Night comes quickly up here."

There was nothing but snow as far as Susan could see. The world was totally quiet. For a moment Susan was afraid to leave the safety of the plane. But then she remembered that they would all freeze to death if they stayed inside it overnight. She jumped down into the snow.

The plane's wing had been torn off in the crash. It lay in the snow beside the plane. Susan looked it over carefully. Suddenly she had an idea. The wing could be used as the roof for a shelter!

She called back towards the plane. "Josh, come here a minute. Do you think we could lift this broken wing? We could use it to make a shelter!"

Josh pulled on his jacket and gloves. Then he jumped down into the snow.

"Let's try it," he said.

Luckily the wing had not been buried in the

snow. Josh and Susan began to pull on it. It was lighter than they had thought! It was easy to drag it away from the plane.

"How about here?" Susan asked. They were about twenty feet from the plane.

"That should be far enough away. There can't be danger of a gas fire now," Josh said. "I'll get a shovel from the plane. Then we can start digging the shelter."

Josh was back in a moment with the shovel.

"We'll have to take turns with it," Susan said. "But the snow is soft and we can dig with our hands, too. We don't have a lot of time. It's getting dark fast. And the wind's coming up."

It was slow going. The hole just didn't seem to be getting any bigger. They dug faster, taking turns with the shovel. Finally they had dug out a space that was about three feet deep.

"It's deep enough," Susan said. "Now we just have to make it wider."

The sky was growing darker by the minute. The wind swept down through the wide valley of snow. Josh and Susan kept on digging.

"That should do it," Josh said finally. "Now let's pull the wing over on top of the hole." He and Susan each grabbed hold of a side of the wing. They dragged it over the hole. It covered half the space. The uncovered part of the hole would be for the fire.

"Not bad! It'll do for right now, at least. Let's just hope we don't get a snowstorm," Josh said.

"I wonder how long we'll be here." Susan looked up at the black sky. "Josh, I'm afraid we're going to have to go for help ourselves. That's the only way we're going to be rescued."

"Let's wait a day or so, Susan. Maybe they'll send a search plane."

"*Who* will send a search plane? No one even knows we're missing. Dad was just about to radio the Steel Ridge airport when the storm hit. I wish someone at Steel Ridge was expecting us. They would have reported us missing by now."

"I guess you're right. But don't say anything to Mom and Dad yet about going for help. We'll get them settled in the shelter first," Josh said. "Let's go back to the plane. We need to get some stuff to start the fire with."

It was dark inside the plane now. Susan could see the glow of her parents' flashlight as she climbed aboard. Dave and Diane looked at their children. There was fear in their eyes. Susan had never seen this before. It was a scary feeling.

CHAPTER 4

Pain

Susan climbed up to the cockpit of the plane. "We've dug out a shelter," she told her parents. "Now we're going to build a fire in it. We're almost ready to bring you out."

"You and Josh have been terrific," Dave said. His voice sounded very tired. He was trying his best to sound cheerful.

"Susan, let me help. I'll get some food together. I'm afraid a lot of it was ruined in the crash, though," Diane said.

Susan felt a chill go down her spine. She hadn't really thought about food yet. She had been so worried about just keeping warm. But they would have to have food. If they didn't, they would not last long on this mountain.

Susan tried to keep her voice cheerful. "Well, let's hope the good stuff made it through the crash! While you see about the food, Josh and I will make the fire."

"Look at this! We've got ready-to-burn logs," Josh said. "Great! Good thing you brought them along for the ski cabin, Mom."

"I wish it was more than half a box. I used the other half up at home," Diane said.

"They'll do for a few hours," Susan said. "But we're going to need wood."

"Where are we going to get some?" Josh asked. "There isn't a tree in sight."

"We're up too high on the mountain for trees. We'll have to go down lower to find some wood. First, let's get the fire started," Susan said.

Wood for the fire. Another problem they hadn't thought about. What if they had to go for miles looking for it? If all else failed, Susan knew they could start burning things from the plane: pillows, seats, and carpet. Their lives might depend on that fire.

Josh and Susan jumped down from the plane. They carried the box of ready-logs. The wind roared in their faces. It felt good to step down into the shelter.

"We're really away from the wind here," Susan said. "I'm glad we dug it this deep." She knelt in the snow. Then she and Josh tore up little pieces of newspaper. They put them underneath the ready-log. Then Josh lit a match. He touched it to the pile of paper. The tiny flame almost died as a gust of wind rushed through the shelter. But it did not die. It came to life and grew larger. Soon it wrapped itself around the ready-logs. Suddenly the night and the shelter seemed friendlier. Susan and Josh sat for a moment watching their fire burn. They knew it could not last for more than a few hours. It was going to need wood. They knew they couldn't allow the fire to go out. They ran to the plane to get their parents.

Dave and Diane were ready to go. They had put on their ski jackets. Diane had made a pile of blankets and sleeping bags. A small box of food sat by the door.

"We're ready to go," Diane said. Susan knew her mother was trying to sound braver than she felt.

"There's not much food left," Diane said. "All the glass bottles and jars broke in the crash. There's enough for a couple of days, though." Diane looked at Susan as if to say, "By then we'll be rescued, right?"

Susan gave her mother a hug. Then she turned to her father. "Josh and I are going to make a seat for you with our arms, Dad. That's how we'll get you out to the shelter. We'll be careful of your leg. Don't worry."

"Just tell me what to do. I'm ready," Dave said.

Josh and Susan turned Dave's seat sideways. Then they faced each other and bent down. They locked their hands together to make a seat.

"Dad, can you scoot forward in your seat? Then Mom can help pull you into our arms," Josh said.

"I'll try," Dave said. He held his right leg out straight. Then he pushed against the back of the seat with his hands.

"Oh, no!" Dave's face went white with pain as he tried to move.

Susan felt sick with fear. What if this made Dad's leg worse? What if he never walks again? But then she asked herself, "Which is worse, not walking or freezing to death?"

CHAPTER 5

Search in the Night

"Can you try it once more, Dad?" Susan felt terrible. It was awful to see her father in such pain.

This time Dave moved more slowly. Diane stood beside him, holding the flashlight. With one final push, Dave moved off of his seat. Susan and Josh caught him neatly in the chair they made with their arms.

"Great going, Dad!" Josh said. "Can you put your arms around our shoulders?"

They started carrying their father towards the plane door. Diane used the flashlight to show the way.

Getting their father out the plane door was going to be tricky, Susan knew. But there was no choice. He had to get to the shelter.

"Mom, please unroll a sleeping bag. We want you to pull the bag up over Dad's legs," Susan said. "Then climb down and be ready by the door. We're going to lower Dad to you feet first. We'll be holding his arms."

"OK," Diane said. She began to gently pull the sleeping bag over Dave's legs. She worked very slowly. She was careful not to press on his right leg. Dave held his breath. But he never cried out. Diane jumped down to the ground.

"OK, you can start letting him down now," Diane said.

"You won't have his whole weight to hold, Mom," Josh told her. "We'll be holding his upper body. And the bag will help balance his weight."

Josh and Susan were stooping in the plane's doorway. Dave was still in their arms. Susan felt as though her arms were about to break off.

"We're going to lower you down to Mom now," Susan told her father. "We won't let go of your arms, though. Don't worry."

"Lower away!" Dave said. Susan knew he was trying to sound brave.

Dave's arms slipped off Josh and Susan's shoulders. Then his children grabbed him under his arms. They let him slowly slide down to Diane, who held the end of the sleeping bag. Josh and Susan grabbed the top corners of the bag. Now Dave was being lowered in a kind of hammock.

"There we go! Gently, gently. OK, Mom, let's lower him slowly to the ground," Josh said. He and Susan still held the top of the sleeping bag. They slowly let themselves slip to the ground. Dave was gently laid down on the snow.

"Great job! I barely felt anything," Dave said. He smiled up at his family.

"Let's head for the shelter," Susan said. "Mom, you and I will hold onto the bottom of the sleeping bag. Josh will carry the top. We'll follow him."

The wind roared around them as they walked to the shelter.

Hooray, the fire's still going, Susan thought. They could see its cheerful glow in the dark.

They slowly lowered Dave into the shelter. Then they made him comfortable under the wing.

"This is terrific," Dave said. "Using the wing was a great idea!"

"It's really warm in here." Diane sat down on a blanket beside Dave's sleeping bag.

The fire was burning very low now.

"We've got to go look for wood," Josh said. "First I'll go get the ax from the plane. I'll bring the food and sleeping bags, too." He ran to the plane.

"You'll have to watch the fire while we're gone," Susan said. "There are three ready-logs left. Don't use them until you have to."

"I'm afraid for you two to go off like this," Diane said. "What if you get lost? What if something happens to one of you?"

"Nothing's going to happen. And we won't get lost. Josh has an extra compass from the plane. Besides, we probably won't have to go far to find some wood." Susan wished she really believed this.

"Why don't you wait till morning to leave?" Dave asked.

"We don't have time to wait. We're going to run out of ready-logs soon," Susan said. How she wished they *could* wait until morning. She wasn't sure she was ready to go out into the cold, dark night.

"Well, at least eat something before you start," Diane said. "Here comes Josh with the food."

"We'll grab some candy bars," Josh said as he set down the box of food. "When we get back, we'll cook up something."

"We'll be taking your flashlight, Dad. Are there any extra batteries?" Susan asked.

"No," Dave answered. "I was going to buy more at Steel Ridge. I wish we had them now!"

"We'll just have to use this very carefully," Susan said as she picked up the flashlight.

"Let's get going," Josh said. He and Susan told their parents good-bye. Then they set off across the snow. They headed down the mountain. After awhile they turned and looked back towards the shelter. It was a tiny glowing spot. Josh and Susan felt good that their parents were warm and safe by the fire. But it would not last much longer. They hurried on into the night down the mountain.

The wind was getting stronger. It was coming straight up the mountain into Josh and Susan's faces. Susan kept her face down and followed Josh's footprints in the snow. If only they would come to some trees! How far would they have to walk? Susan raised her eyes to look ahead. All she could see was snow stretching far ahead. She kept following Josh. Her stomach growled. She knew she should have eaten more than a candy bar before leaving.

Suddenly she heard him yelling. He was pointing to something ahead. Susan tried to see what it was.

"Trees! I'm sure of it," Josh yelled.

Then Susan saw them too. They stood tall and dark on the ridge ahead. Never had a tree looked so good! They hurried ahead.

"First let's look for fallen logs," Josh said. "We can cut them up more easily."

Several fallen trees lay on the ground. Josh started to chop one up with his ax. Susan shone the flashlight on the log for him. The wind died down. The night was cold and still. The sound of the ax seemed to echo out over the whole mountain.

Soon Josh had two nice piles of wood stacked up.

"Let's head back with these," Susan said. "We can come back in the morning."

They each picked up an armful of wood. Then they set out for the shelter. The wood was heavy. It was going to take a long time to get back.

Suddenly they heard a new sound. They both shivered. It was a long, slow, ghostly howl. Wolves!

"Josh, where are they? Are they close?" Susan cried. She shook with fright. She had never thought about wolves on the mountain. Here was another enemy to be faced along with the cold and little food.

"They're off to the right of us," Josh said. "I don't think they'll bother us. I've heard they're afraid of people."

The howling began again. It seemed to be getting closer. How I *wish* we were back at the shelter, Susan thought. The fire would keep the wolves away.

Susan kept following Josh across the mountainside. The howling went on and on.

Suddenly Josh stopped. "Don't move, Susan," he said.

There in the darkness were six pairs of yellow eyes.

CHAPTER 6

Fear on the Mountain

The wolves did not move closer. They sat and watched Josh and Susan. Their bright yellow eyes never seemed to blink. Susan and Josh did not move. They stared at the wolves.

Josh finally said, "Hand me the flashlight, Susan. I'm going to try something."

Suddenly he shone the flashlight right at the wolves. They jumped back. They walked back and forth growling, watching Josh and Susan. Josh shone the light straight at them again. Then they began to move away into the dark.

"They're going!" Susan whispered.

"We hope. They may just move farther back. I bet they'll keep watching us," Josh said.

Sure enough, the wolves stopped moving. They were about thirty feet away.

"Let's get going. *Real* slow. I don't think they'll attack. They're just looking us over," Josh said.

Suddenly he shone the flashlight at the wolves.

They started walking again. They each carried an armful of wood. Josh hooked the flashlight into his belt and kept it lit.

The wolves did not move. They just stood there watching.

"I think we're OK," Susan called ahead softly to Josh.

"They're following us. Just keep walking,"

Josh said in a low voice.

On and on they walked across the snowy mountain, not a sound except their footsteps. And the wolves kept following.

Suddenly Josh and Susan saw the bright glow of a fire ahead. The shelter! They were almost there. Only now did Susan dare turn around. She did not see the wolves.

"They're gone, Josh!" she cried.

"They'll be back," her brother answered.

Diane stood by the fire waving.

"You're back! We were so worried. You were gone so long." She hugged her children tightly.

"We found wood! It will last us at least through tomorrow," Josh said.

"How are you feeling, Mom? Dad, how's your leg?" Susan sat down with her father under the wing. She hoped Josh wouldn't tell her parents about the wolves. At least not tonight.

"Not too good. The pain's worse," Dave said.

"Let's try putting your leg up," Susan said to her father. "That might help to stop the pain." She rolled up a blanket and carefully put it under Dave's leg.

I need to talk to Josh, Susan thought to herself. We've got to make a plan about going for help. We'll talk after Mom and Dad are asleep. I know Dad will say he doesn't want us to go. But there isn't anything else to do.

"Maybe some plane will spot our fire tonight," Diane said. "It should be easy to see a fire this big."

"How I wish!" Dave said. "But this isn't a regular flying route. Planes don't usually go over these mountains. I was taking a shortcut over them to save time. We'd have been OK if that storm hadn't hit."

"Your map is in the plane, isn't it, Dad?" Josh asked. "I'm going to go get it." He ran off towards the plane.

"I bet you kids could use something to eat," Diane said. "You've had nothing but those candy bars. Dad and I heated some soup in these tin coffee cups. Want me to heat you up some, too?" she asked Susan.

"I'd love it. The hotter, the better." Susan knew how good the hot soup would feel inside her.

Josh came back with the map. He brought the flashlight over and sat down beside his father. Susan joined them. They unfolded the map and laid it on Dave's sleeping bag. Dave studied the map for a long time. Then he put his finger down on a spot.

"Here. I think we came down here. I remember seeing this peak just before the storm." Dave pointed to a mountain marked "Dawson" on the map.

"So we're right in here somewhere," Josh said. He put his finger on a large white space underneath Mt. Dawson.

"Where would the nearest town be?" Diane asked.

Susan hated to hear the answer. The map seemed to show nothing but wilderness.

"Darcyville is the closest," Dave said. He pointed to a small dot on the map.

"A long way," Josh said. "What would you say, Dad? Forty miles?"

"About that. Maybe a little more."

"Dad. Mom. Nobody's going to be looking for us up here. We've got to get help soon. Susan and I want to go down the mountain. I know we could do it." Josh looked at his parents.

"No way. Let you go forty miles down this mountain? Do you know how long that would take you? You'd never make it. We'll wait here in the shelter. A search plane will come along. I'm sure of it," Dave said.

"Dad's right. We couldn't let you go off alone. We'd never see you again. You'd get lost and freeze to death." Diane put her arms around Susan.

"But, Dad, what about your leg? You've got to get to a doctor. If you don't get your leg set, you might never walk again. And if we stay here, we all might die of hunger," Josh said.

"Please let us go, Dad. At least this way there's a chance of bringing help. We'll get lots of wood for you and Mom before we leave. You'd be OK till we got back. They could land a helicopter here to rescue you," Susan said.

Dave looked at his children for a long time. Then he stared out at the fire.

"Wait a day. We'll see if a rescue plane spots us tomorrow. We'll keep a big fire going all day long. If nobody comes, then you two can start early the next morning," Dave said. "What do you think, Diane?"

"I'm scared. I'm afraid to let them go. Wait at least two more days here, kids. A plane will find us. I know it," Diane said.

"The longer we wait, the bigger the danger for Dad's leg," Josh said. "We should start down as soon as possible."

"Stay tomorrow. If nothing happens, then you can go. But we hate for you to do it."

"In the morning we'll go back for more wood," Josh said.

"We'll leave you plenty. Enough to last till we come back for you," Susan told her parents.

"How's the food supply?" Josh asked.

Diane started looking through the box of supplies. "About ten cans of soup. Some packets of cocoa, some apples. A couple packages of crackers and cookies. A few candy bars. That's it."

Suddenly they heard the howl of the wolves.

"What was that? Wolves? Could there be wolves up here?" Diane's voice shook with fear.

"Yes, they're wolves all right. A few of them followed Susan and me back here. They're afraid of the fire, though. As long as it keeps burning, we're OK," Josh said.

Dave pulled Susan close and hugged her. How could he let his children go off alone down this mountain? A search plane *had* to come tomorrow.

CHAPTER 7

Getting Ready

Josh sat up most of the night to keep the fire going. He knew they must never let it go out. The wolves had stayed near the shelter all night. When dawn came they slowly drifted away.

"You get some sleep now," Susan told Josh when she woke up. "I'll watch the fire. You've had a long night."

Josh lay down in his sleeping bag. Dave and Diane were still asleep under the wing.

"Going down the mountain is going to be rough," Josh said to Susan. "I can go alone if you don't want to do it."

"Are you kidding? I'm going with you. Two of us have much more of a chance than one," Susan said. She threw more wood into the fire. "Later on we'd better go get more wood. We'll have to make a couple of trips. Mom and Dad are going to need a big supply."

They kept a huge fire burning all day at the shelter. But no search planes flew overhead. Josh and Susan made three trips to gather wood. They felt certain they would be leaving the next morning. They took their suitcases off the plane. Extra jeans, sweaters, and socks were put aside for the trip.

Diane helped Josh and Susan pack their supplies. There was no knapsack to use. Susan's book bag would carry their food and clothes.

"I'd better give you the can opener," Diane told them. "I'll open our soup cans now. Then I'll just set them in the snow. The cold air will keep the soup from spoiling."

Josh and Susan packed six cans of soup in their bag. Little bags of cocoa and two drinking cups also went in. Crackers, cookies, apples, and candy bars went in last.

"Do you have my compass?" Dave asked. "And the map?"

"We've got both, Dad. And the first aid kit," Susan answered.

"How about a knife and extra matches?" Dave was checking through their bag.

"In my pocket," Josh said.

"Promise us you won't keep walking once it's dark," Dave said. "Make camp and start a fire."

"We promise," Susan told her parents. She knew she wanted to be close to a fire when night came.

"You kids had better get to bed," Dave said. "You'll want to get an early start tomorrow." He still had his leg up to help the pain. But he hadn't told his family that his leg had begun to swell.

They were all awake at dawn. Diane fixed hot cocoa for the family. The box of cookies was passed around. Everyone took just two.

"We'll be thinking of you every minute," Diane said. There were tears in her eyes. "Please be very, very careful."

"You, too, Mom and Dad. You take care. And remember to keep your leg up, Dad," Susan said. She tried to make her voice sound cheerful. But there was a heavy feeling in her chest.

Josh and Susan hugged their parents. Then they quickly left the shelter.

CHAPTER 8

Terror in the Forest

By noon Josh and Susan had left the high country behind. Now they were deep in the mountain forest. There was no trail to follow. They just kept heading downhill. On the map, Darcyville was supposed to be straight south. But no one knew for sure exactly where the plane had crashed. Susan kept a close watch on the compass. They had to keep heading south. Sooner or later they had to come to a town, a road, something.

It was slow going through the forest. The snow had drifted deep among the trees. Josh and Susan waded through three-foot drifts. Their legs soon felt numb. Their jeans were soaked from the cold wet snow. The wind roared down through the trees.

Finally they reached the bank of a stream. There were wide rock ledges all along the water.

Josh and Susan crawled in under one to rest. They were both soaked to the skin. Susan couldn't stop shivering. Her lips were blue. She suddenly felt terribly tired all over. She felt as though she didn't care about going on.

"I'd better build a fire. We've got to get you warmed up," Josh said to Susan.

Josh soon had a nice blaze going under the rock ledge. He made Susan put on dry socks and jeans. Then he heated cocoa for them both. Susan's shivering slowly stopped.

They followed the stream all afternoon. The wind howled down the mountain at their backs. After awhile they came to a deer trail that followed the stream. This made walking much easier. But the forest seemed endless.

It began to get dark. Susan started thinking about her parents back at the shelter. She hoped they had a good fire going.

Then the howling began. It seemed to be all around them. Then they knew that the wolves had been following them. Susan felt sick with fear.

"Josh, we've got to stop and make a fire. Fast!"

They both looked wildly for wood. They made a small pile and then tucked pine needles underneath. The howling of the wolves was getting closer all the time. Josh and Susan blew on the tiny sparks. At last, a tiny flame! The flame grew bigger. The night seemed suddenly brighter, warmer. They sat very close to the fire. Then they saw the eyes. The wolves stood among the trees and watched them.

"I don't like this," Josh stared at the wolves. "I don't trust them."

"Josh, look!" Susan cried. One of the wolves was coming closer. Josh grabbed a burning stick from the fire and stood up. He waved the flaming stick as the wolf came closer. Susan watched in horror. The wolf was huge and gray. His yellow eyes stared at Josh.

"Be careful, Josh!" Susan screamed. Josh waved the stick faster and faster at the wolf. Suddenly the wolf stopped coming. He snarled and stared at the flaming stick. Then he turned and ran back into the trees.

"He's gone. They've all gone. He must have been the leader," Josh said. "They could still come back. We'll have to make sure our fire burns all night."

Josh took the first turn at watching the fire. Susan lay in her sleeping bag and looked up at the stars. How many nights will we spend on this

He snarled at the flaming stick.

mountain, she wondered. What if this stream leads us nowhere? Somewhere in the distance a wolf howled.

CHAPTER 9

Trouble on the Trail

Susan woke up cold. The fire had gone out! Josh had fallen asleep.

Susan shook Josh by the shoulder. "Wake up! The fire's out!" Susan started gathering wood. Josh felt awful that he had fallen asleep and let the fire die. He soon had a roaring fire going for breakfast. They had hot cocoa with apples and cookies. Then they packed up and put out the fire.

They followed the stream through the forest all day. Nothing changed. The forest was as thick and dark as ever.

That night they took turns watching the fire. The wolves howled far in the distance.

The sky was gray in the morning. "It's going to snow," Josh said as they packed up to leave. "We'd better move fast. Maybe the bottom of the mountain is close."

They were still following the stream. And the forest was as thick as ever. But there was a change. Now there were more rocks.

Maybe these rocks mean we're close to the bottom of the mountain, Susan thought to herself. If only this were true! She was tired. Her whole body ached. The bottoms of her feet hurt terribly.

Suddenly Josh fell! He had tripped over a large rock on the path. He sat on the ground holding his ankle. His face was white with pain.

"Josh!" Susan knelt beside her brother.

"My ankle! It really hurts!" Josh's ankle was already swollen.

"Don't move. Stay right here," Susan said. She knew they were in trouble. Big trouble. Her mind felt numb. She moved without thinking. She gathered wood for a fire. She wrapped Josh's ankle with one of her socks. All the while she felt terror growing inside of her.

"You've got to leave me here and keep going," Josh said. "I'll be OK."

"I can't leave you here, Josh!" Susan cried. "You'll freeze to death. And what about the wolves?"

"Just leave a big pile of wood right beside me. I can keep a fire going. I can heat up food. If you don't go on, we'll never get help. I won't be able to walk on this ankle for days."

"There's only one way that I'll go," Susan said slowly. "That's if I can come back to you in two days if I haven't found help. You'll need more wood by then."

"OK. It's a deal. Let's hope we're near the bottom of this mountain." Josh looked up at the gray sky and knew it would soon snow. But he said nothing to Susan. She would never leave him if a snowstorm was coming.

Susan gathered armfuls of wood. She made a huge pile beside Josh. Then she carefully built a big fire. She opened cans of soup for him and set them in the snow. Then she piled up what was left of the rest of the food.

"Hey! What about you? You've got to eat," Josh told her. "Put some of these things back in your bag. And take the map with you."

Susan didn't want Josh to know how scared she was. Just after the crash, it had seemed so easy to be brave. She had felt in control of things. Why did she feel so scared now?

CHAPTER 10

Into the Blizzard

The forest was a ghostly quiet. Susan's boots made no sound on the snowy path. She walked carefully.

The trees were not so close together now. The forest was brighter. Please, she thought to herself, make this mountain end. Suddenly she felt something wet hit her face. She looked up. Snow! The gray sky was thick with it. She thought of Josh. She must go back to him. What if he were buried by the blizzard? No, she told herself. I've got to keep going. Maybe I'm near a road. I can't turn back now.

She walked faster through the forest. The blizzard was all around her. It was blinding her. Suddenly Susan smelled something in the air. It was smoke! Was there a camp nearby? There must be!

Susan started to run towards the smell. She was

no longer careful of falling. She just kept running. The smell of smoke was growing stronger.

There it was. She nearly ran into it. It's a cabin! Smoke was coming out of the chimney. There must be someone inside. She ran up to the door and pounded on it.

"Please. Is anybody here? Please help me!" she cried.

There it was. It's a cabin! Smoke was coming out of the chimney. There must be someone inside.

The door swung open. Susan looked up at a man in a green uniform. He quickly pulled her inside the house.

"You're nearly frozen! Where have you come from?" the forest ranger asked. "Come inside quickly and get warm."

Susan warmed her hands over the pot-bellied stove as she told Ranger Hill her story. After that, things moved very quickly. First, Susan and the ranger looked at her father's map. She had pointed to where she thought her parents were. The ranger had got on his radio to the air rescue team right away.

"They'll find your parents and take them to a hospital," Ranger Hill said. "I'll go after your brother."

Now, much later, Susan stood at the cabin window. She was waiting for Ranger Hill and Josh. She looked out into the blizzard. Still no sign of them. Was the ranger having trouble finding Josh?

Susan looked out into the blizzard. Still no sign of the ranger and Josh. When would they get here? Maybe the ranger couldn't find Josh.

Suddenly she spotted a figure coming through the snow. It was Ranger Hill. He was pulling a sled behind him. A bundle lay on it. The bundle was very still. Susan raced out the cabin door. She was almost afraid to look at Josh's face. But she did. And he was grinning up at her.

"Hi, Susan! Boy, is this the way to come down the mountain!" Josh said.

"Josh! You're OK!" Susan hugged her brother. "I was so worried when I saw you lying on the sled."

"I'm all tied up like a mummy. I can't move," Josh said.

"Did Ranger Hill tell you Mom and Dad are being rescued? The helicopter should be up there by now," Susan said happily.

"Hey, Susan! Better get inside! Don't you know you have bare feet?" laughed Ranger Hill.

"Who cares!" Susan yelled and raced inside to the fire.